Usborne Farmyard Tales

Sticker Learning Book
Letters to copy

Illustrated by Stephen Cartwright

Edited by Lisa Miles
Designed by Joe Pedley

Series editor: Jenny Tyler
Handwriting consultant: Rosemary Sassoon

Line illustrations by Guy Smith
With thanks to Heather Amery and Jo Goodall

I found the duck!

A little yellow duck is hidden on every two pages.
When you have found the duck, you can put one of these stickers on the page.

For advice on how to use this book, see Notes for Parents on page 16.

This is Apple Tree Farm. Mr. and Mrs. Boot live here with their children, Poppy and Sam, and a dog called Rusty.

Draw in the clouds.

Find the stickers to see who else lives here.

Ted, who works on the farm

Woolly the sheep

Curly the pig

Draw over the dotted lines and find the stickers to complete the picture.

Draw over these letters. Copy them to fill the line.

l i t l i t

Now do the same with these smaller letters.

l i t l i t

Draw over the wavy line and keep it going to reach the boat. Find the stickers too.

Draw over the wavy line. Make it reach the duck.

Draw over these letters. Copy them to fill the line.

u y j u

Draw over the wavy line. Make it reach the fish.

Draw over these letters. Copy them to fill the line.

4

Draw over the wavy line and keep it going to show where Poppy's ball bounced.

Draw over where Sam's ball bounced.

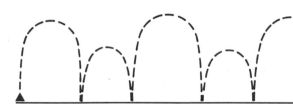

Draw over these letters. Copy them to fill the line.

n m n

Draw over where Rusty's ball bounced.

Draw over these letters. Copy them to fill the line.

n m n

5

These people are all driving to Apple Tree Farm. Draw over their tracks. Find the stickers too.

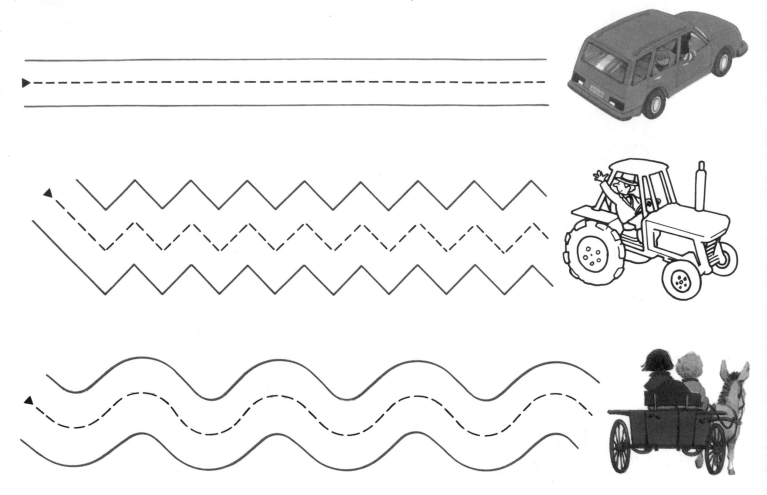

Draw over these letters. Copy them to fill the line.

h r h

Now do the same with these smaller letters.

h r h

What are all these people doing? Draw over
their tracks.

Draw over these letters. Copy them to fill the line.

b p k b

Now do the same with these smaller letters.

b p k b

Draw a row of round apples.

Draw circles to give the frogs some eyes.

Draw over these letters. Copy them to fill the line.

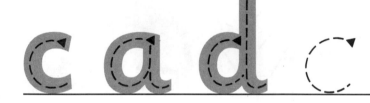

Now give these smaller frogs some eyes.

Draw over these letters. Copy them to fill the line.

I found the duck!

I found the duck!

I found the duck!

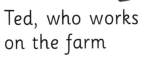

Ted, who works on the farm

I found the duck!

Zoo

Lake

Woolly the sheep

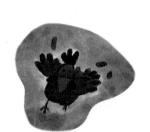

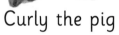

Curly the pig

Park

Mr. Boot is taking Poppy and Sam on a journey. Follow the car to see where they went.

1. Draw a line to take the car from Apple Tree Farm to the Campsite. Go past the Market.

Market

Apple Tree Farm

Park

Forest

Campsite

3. Now draw a line from the Park to the Show. Go past the Zoo.

Lake

2. Draw another line to take the car from the Campsite to the Park.

Show

Zoo

4. Now draw a line to take the car back to Apple Tree Farm.

Find the stickers to complete the picture.

The barn is on fire! Draw over the firefighters' hoses. Find the stickers.

Draw over these letters. Copy them to fill the line.

g q g

Now do the same with these smaller letters.

g q g

Draw over these letters. Copy them to fill the line.

Now do the same with these smaller letters.

Draw over the line to help the sheepdog round up Woolly and her friends. Find the stickers.

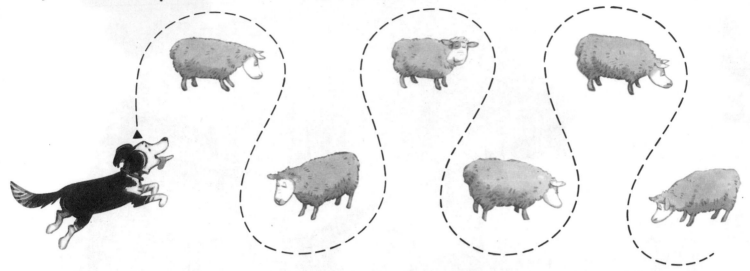

Draw over this pattern to reach the lost sheep.

Draw over the letters. Copy them to fill the line.

Now do the same with these smaller letters.

Poppy and Sam are chasing Curly. Draw over the line they make as they run around the buckets.

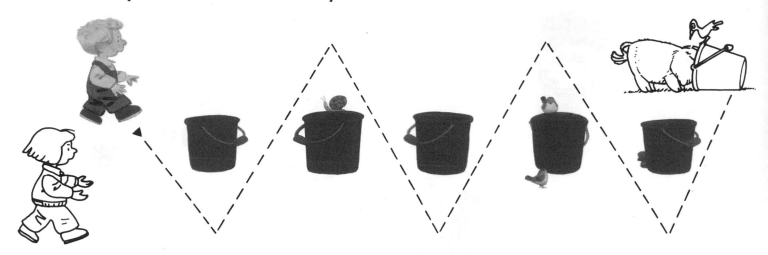

Draw over this pattern to reach the hungry piglets.

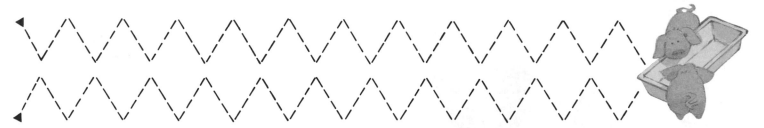

Draw over the letters. Copy them to fill the line.

V W V

Now do the same with these smaller letters.

Look at Poppy and Sam's toys. Draw over the lines and find the stickers to complete the picture.

Draw over the letters. Copy them to fill the line.

Now do the same with these smaller letters.

Now you can write all the letters. Capital letters are used at the beginning of names, like this:

Poppy and Sam

Ask someone to write your name for you here.

_____

Now copy your name below.

_____

NOTES FOR PARENTS

This activity book will help young children to start developing a clear handwriting style. Here are a few points to help you and your child get the most from this book.

Children should hold their pens and pencils lightly, between their first two fingers and thumb. Help them to hold the pencil like this, but make sure that they can make free movements with their hand. If a child is left-handed, it is important to make sure that he or she is following the activities from left to right and from top to bottom.

By doing the activities with your child, you can demonstrate basic concepts, such as writing from left to right. Arrows show where to start each one. Encourage children to make free movements and help them to choose different pens and pencils. Let them do the activities several times and don't worry too much about neatness.

Make sure that your child is still enjoying each activity. You can always come back to them later. You could add activities of your own, such as making patterns with sand or glitter, or helping children to write their names on letters or birthday cards.

Wherever you see a black and white picture in the book, there is a sticker to match.

The letters

Throughout the book, there are letters for your child to draw over and copy. They are introduced in groups of related shapes, rather than in alphabetical order. The small letters of the alphabet are given first, because children learning to read and write begin with these. Capital letters are shown next to the relevant small letters at the end of the book. When writing letters for children, use capitals only where you would normally, such as at the beginning of their names.

The letters to copy are shown large and then small. This will help children to improve their pencil control, while learning the forms of the letters. Arrows show the starting points for each letter. Make sure that your child follows the directions shown below for the strokes. Each letter should be written in one flowing movement, apart from f, i, j, t and x, which have two strokes.

a b c d e f g h i j k l m
n o p q r s t u v w x y z

16